P9-BIU-264

ONCE UPON a TIME TALES

retold by
Corinne Denan

illustrated by
Karin Lidbeck

Troll Associates

Copyright © 1980 by Troll Associates, Mahwah, N.J.

All rights reserved. No portion of this book may be reproduced in any form, electronic or mechanical, including photocopying, recording, or information storage and retrieval systems, without prior written permission from the publisher. Printed in the United States of America.

Library of Congress # 79-66337
ISBN 0-89375-340-8/0-89375-339-4 (pb)

CONTENTS

The Three Spinners

Once upon a time, long ago, there was a girl who was very lazy. All day long, she would sit at the spinning wheel, but she would not spin. Nothing anyone could do would make her spin flax into yarn.

One day her mother lost all patience, and cried, "If you will not start spinning, I will take a stick and beat you!" But still the girl refused. And so her mother gave her such a beating that her cries filled the house and spilled out into the street.

Now it so happened that the Queen was passing by at that very moment. She stopped, and asked what the girl had done to deserve such a beating.

The mother was too ashamed to tell the Queen of the girl's laziness. So instead of the truth, she said, "I am beating my daughter to stop her from spinning. She spins all day, and she spins all night, and I cannot find enough flax to keep up with her!"

"Then she shall come with me," replied the Queen. "I have more than enough flax at my castle, and no one to spin it. She shall spin to her heart's content."

The girl's mother agreed. At last, she would be rid of her lazy daughter. So the girl climbed into the carriage with the Queen, and rode in silence to the castle.

There, she was taken inside and shown a spinning wheel in the middle of a large room. Beyond that room was a larger room. And beyond that, an even larger room. And each room was filled from floor to ceiling with flax.

"Now you can spin all you like," remarked the Queen. "That will make you very happy, I am sure. And when you have spun all this flax into yarn, you shall have my eldest son as your bridegroom."

When the Queen left, the girl looked at the mountains of flax in the three rooms. "This is enough to keep a hundred spinners busy for a hundred years," she thought. "I would not even know where to begin." Then she sat down at the spinning wheel and began to cry.

After three days, the Queen looked in to see how the girl was coming along with her spinning. "Why, you have not even begun!" she exclaimed. "Is anything wrong?"

But the girl only shook her head sadly.

"Ah," said the Queen, "I see you are homesick! But that will pass when you begin to spin."

When the Queen left, the girl was alone again with the spinning wheel and the mountains of flax. She did not know what to do, so she did nothing. She just sat by the window and day-dreamed.

By and by, she saw three old women passing by. The first had one foot that was much larger and flatter than the other. The second had a huge lower lip that hung down to her chin. The third had a thumb as big as an apple, and just as red. All three women stopped beneath the girl's window and asked what was wrong.

"When I spin all this flax into yarn, I can marry a Prince," explained the girl. "But I don't know how to begin."

"We can help you," said the woman with the big thumb. "But if we do, you must promise us something in return."

"I would give you anything," cried the girl, "if I had anything to give. But I have nothing— nothing at all."

"Then you must invite us to the wedding feast," said the old woman with the huge foot.

"And you must invite us to eat at your table," said the woman with the drooping lip.

"And you must call us your cousins," added the woman with the big thumb. "If you promise these things, then we shall help you."

The girl gave her promise, and began to clear a space for the women to do their spinning.

As soon as they were inside the room, they set to work. The first drew out the thread and used her large flat foot to work the treadle that turned the spinning wheel. The second moistened the thread on her huge, droopy lip. Then the third used her enormous thumb to twist the thread and to rap on the table at which she worked. And every time she rapped on the table, a great pile of beautifully spun yarn fell to the floor.

All day long, and into the night, the sound of the spinning wheel filled the room. The three spinners worked without tiring.

In the morning, when the Queen came to see how the spinning was coming along, the three spinners hid in the next room. The Queen could hardly believe her eyes. The first room was filled with the most beautiful yarn she had ever seen. And the girl was sound asleep next to the spinning wheel. Of course, the Queen thought the girl had been up all night, spinning.

When the Queen left, the three spinners set to work in the second room. They worked all day

and far into the night. By morning, the flax in the second room had been spun into yarn, and the spinners hid in the third room.

The Queen peeked in and saw the girl asleep on the yarn. "She must have been up all night," thought the Queen.

After the Queen had left, the three spinners set to work in the third room. Soon, they had spun the last of the flax into yarn.

"We have kept our promise," they said to the girl. "Now you must keep yours."

"You must invite us to your wedding," said the first.

"And let us eat at your table," said the second.

"And call us your cousins," added the third.

Then they left the girl standing by the spinning wheel, surrounded by the piles of newly spun yarn.

That very afternoon, the Queen announced the wedding plans. The King declared a holiday. And the Prince rejoiced at the thought of having such a lovely and skillful bride.

"I have three cousins," said the girl. "They have been so kind to me, that I must invite them to the wedding feast."

"Of course," agreed the Queen.

"And they must sit at the table with us," added the girl.

"Of course," replied the Prince.

"Then it is settled," announced the King.

The wedding was held the next day. When the three women arrived at the wedding feast, the bride welcomed them at the door.

"Come in, dear cousins," she said. "Come and sit with us at our table."

Everyone stared at the first woman's huge foot, at the second woman's drooping lip, and at the third woman's enormous thumb. Then the groom looked at his bride again, and thought to himself, "She is lovely, yet her cousins are exceedingly ugly. How can this be?"

Then he went up to the first woman and said, "How is it that your foot is so broad and flat?"

And the woman answered, "From working the treadle as I spin."

The groom went to the second woman and asked, "How is it that your lower lip is so large and droopy?"

"From moistening the thread as I spin," she replied.

And to the third woman, the groom said, "How is it that your thumb is so exceedingly large?"

"From twisting the thread as I spin," she said.

Then the groom looked at his lovely bride and announced, "From this time forward, my wife shall never touch a spinning wheel again."

And so, for the rest of her days, the girl who would not spin . . . did not spin.

The Lost Princesses

One cold winter long, long ago, a King and Queen were riding in their sleigh. The Queen brushed against a hanging branch and cut her finger. Drops of blood fell upon the white snow.

"How beautiful the bright red looks upon the white," said the Queen. "I wish that we might have a daughter so lovely."

At that moment, an old woman appeared. "Your wish will be granted," she said. "But if your daughter steps outside the castle during her first twelve years, a terrible misfortune shall befall you."

A short time later, a beautiful daughter was born to the royal couple.

The next winter the King and Queen were out riding in their sleigh. Once again the Queen cut her finger. She made the same wish. The old woman appeared and said the same words. And a second beautiful daughter was born.

The third year, the same thing happened. And a third beautiful daughter was born.

The King and Queen dearly loved their three children, and they took care to heed the words of the old woman. But as the girls grew older, they longed to go outside and play in the palace gardens.

But the Queen said sadly, "Until you are each twelve years old, you must never step outside of these palace walls."

Now the youngest Princess was the most beautiful of the three daughters. And of the three, her desire to go outside was the strongest. Each day, she would watch from her window, as a young boy, named Roland, worked in the garden. He was a homeless lad whom the King had befriended. Roland would wave to the youngest Princess and show her the beautiful flowers in the garden.

Time passed. The oldest daughter was now nearly twelve and the youngest nearly ten.

It so happened that the King and Queen were invited to a neighboring kingdom for the wedding of their godson. The Queen had never left her children unattended, and she did not wish to go.

"But we cannot refuse to attend the wedding of our godson," said the King. "We will leave our most trusted servants in charge of our daughters."

The Queen reluctantly agreed, and they left for the wedding. The three Princesses waved to them from the castle window. Then the youngest daughter saw her friend Roland in the garden.

"Can't we go outside in the garden for just one moment?" she begged the servants.

And her sisters cried, "Oh please, just for a moment. No one will see us!"

The old servants did not know about the old woman's warning. They had always thought it strange that the girls were kept inside all the time. "Just for a moment," they agreed. "No one will have to know."

For the first time in their lives, the three young girls ran outside in the garden. How beautiful the sun was! How green the grass was! But, as they ran toward Roland, a terrible storm arose. The servants shielded their eyes from the sharp wind. And when they looked again, the three Princesses were gone!

Roland and the servants looked everywhere, but there was no trace of the girls. The servants were so afraid that they ran from the castle and fled the country.

When the Queen heard what had happened, she blamed herself for not taking care of her children. She dressed in a gown of heavy black silk. "I will wear this gown until my daughters re-

turn," she said. "If it is worn out before I see them again, I will go to my grave."

The King could do nothing to change the Queen's mind. Finally, to try to cheer her, he adopted the young boy Roland as their son.

The years passed. Roland grew into a fine young man. But no word of the beautiful Princesses ever reached the castle.

One morning, Roland said to the King and Queen, "Last night I dreamed of the Princesses. I dreamed they were imprisoned in a far-off castle. I must ride out in search of them."

The Queen did not want him to go. "We will only lose you, too," she said. "Besides, it is too late. My dress is nearly worn, and I shall soon die."

But the King told Roland to go. He dressed him in fine armor and gave him a great horse to ride. Then he told two of his most trusted knights to ride with him. The King did not know that the knights were jealous of Roland and would gladly see him dead.

After many months, Roland and the knights came upon a deserted castle, just like the one in his dream. They entered the castle and found a huge pot boiling on the stove. "This looks like soup, and I am very hungry," said one of the knights. But when he looked into the pot, he saw a hand floating in it.

The two knights turned in horror and fled from the castle.

Just then, an ugly dwarf stepped into the kitchen. When he saw Roland, an evil grin appeared on his face, and he said, "More food for the pot, I see."

"You'll have to fight me first," said Roland, drawing his sword.

"We'll see about that," said the dwarf, still grinning. Although the dwarf was small, his magic powers made him very strong. He stepped forward and knocked the sword from Roland's hand. Then he dragged him by the hair to a huge chopping block.

But Roland remained calm. "I could make it easier for you," he said, "but I do not know what you want. Just show me what to do, and I will help you."

"You are stupid, indeed," cried the dwarf. "But since this is your last wish, I will do as you ask."

The evil dwarf knelt on the floor in front of the chopping block. "Just put your head down there," he said.

"I'm afraid I still don't understand what you mean," said Roland.

"You are more than stupid!" the dwarf cried. "Here, like this." And the dwarf put his head on the chopping block.

Quick as lightning, Roland grabbed an axe, and struck at the dwarf with one mighty blow.

At that very instant, the castle vanished with a loud, piercing noise. Roland found himself standing on a hillside. At the edge of the hill stood a great, dark pit. As Roland peered over the edge, the two knights came riding up to him.

"Perhaps the Princesses are down in this pit," said Roland. "Help me to search for them." But the knights refused.

"I will go myself then," said Roland, and he tied a rope tightly around his waist. Then he handed the other end of the rope to the knights.

Slowly, Roland lowered himself into the pit. Never had he seen such darkness. Cobwebs brushed his face. Bat wings fluttered against his cheek. But down and down he went.

Finally, his feet reached bottom. Rats scurried past him. Roland carefully felt his way down a

small passage. At last he came upon a door. He knocked, and it was opened from within.

There before him stood the three lost Princesses. They had grown into young ladies. And they were more beautiful than ever.

"Do you remember me?" asked Roland. "I was the young boy who waved to you from the palace garden."

All three Princesses remembered him, and especially the youngest. Tears of happiness rolled down her cheeks. Suddenly, she remembered the evil dwarf.

"Now you are his prisoner too," she sighed. "He will never let us go."

"Do not fear, Princess," said Roland. "The evil dwarf is no more. And now we must flee this place. Your mother still grieves for you, and at this moment she may be dying."

When the Princesses reached for the rope, the two jealous knights pulled them up to safety. But Roland did not trust the knights. So when they lowered the rope for him, he tied a large rock to the end. The knights pulled on the rope, and the rock rose higher and higher. Then, suddenly, it clattered back down into the pit. The knights had cut the rope. Up on the hillside, the Princesses wept for young Roland. But the knights forced them to return home. "You must tell your parents that we rescued you," said the knights. "If you do not, we will kill you, too."

The Princesses could do nothing but agree. So Roland was left at the bottom of the pit.

There was only one way for Roland to save himself. Somehow he had to climb the steep, slimy walls of the pit. Time and again, he lost his grip, and slipped back down to the bottom.

"I must not give up," he vowed. "If I do not return to the King and Queen, they will never know the truth."

His strength was all but drained, and his hands were raw and bleeding. But at last, Roland reached the top of the pit.

After many days, he arrived at the castle. Disguised as a knight from a strange country, he learned that the jealous knights were planning to marry two of the Princesses.

That evening, a great feast was held. Roland walked into the banquet hall, still wearing his disguise. No one, except the youngest Princess, recognized him.

"I have come to tell you a story," said the strange knight. And he told of how a young man

had rescued three princesses from an evil dwarf and was left to die in a pit. As he neared the end of the story, the youngest Princess ran to him and cried, "This knight tells the truth. For he is Roland. It was he who saved us from the evil dwarf. And it was he who was left in the pit by those two jealous knights!"

The fury of the King was so great that everyone shrank from him. "Hang the cowards!" he shouted. "Hang them at once!"

"No, my husband," said the Queen. "My children have come back to me. Let us have no killing on this most joyous of days."

"Then the knights will be banished from the kingdom forever," said the King. And so it was done.

The very next day, Roland and the youngest Princess were married. And they lived happily ever after, for all of their days.

The Raven

Once there was a Princess who was so restless that her mother could get no peace. One day, when the Queen saw a flock of ravens pass the castle, she cried out, "If only my daughter were a raven and could fly away, at last I would get some rest."

As soon as these words were spoken, the Princess was changed into a raven. She flew out the window and into a dark wood, where she lived for many years. Then one day, a handsome young man happened by.

The raven called out to him, saying, "I was a Princess until I was bewitched. But you can set me free."

"Tell me how," begged the young man.

"You must go deeper into the wood," said the raven. "There, you will come to a house in which an old woman lives. Stay there for three days, but do not eat or drink. Each day, you must stand in the garden and watch for me. The first day, I will come by in a carriage drawn by four white horses. The second day, four red horses will pull the carriage, and on the third day, four black horses.

You must not sleep at all, for if you can stay awake, the enchantment will be broken. But if your eyes should close, I must fly away."

The young man agreed to do what the raven said, and he set off at once for the deepest part of the wood. Soon he came to the house, where the old woman offered him food and drink. He refused them, but the woman would give him no peace.

"You look weary from your journey," she said. "If you will not eat, then at least take a sip from this cup." And at last, the young man gave in and took a drink.

That afternoon, he went into the garden behind the house and watched for the raven. He felt very tired, but he knew he must not sleep. "At least it can do no harm to rest my weary bones," he said. So he lay down, but did not close his eyes.

By the time the raven appeared, however, the young man had fallen asleep. The same thing happened on the second day, and again on the third.

The raven shook him and called to him, but could not awaken him. She left him a jug of cider and a sack filled with bread and meat.

She also placed a golden ring by his side, and left a note that said, "You can do nothing for me here. If you still wish to save me, you must come to the golden castle." Then she flew back to the carriage and rode off.

Before long, the young man awakened and knew at once what had happened. He was sad, because he knew he had failed to break the enchantment. But when he found the ring and the note, he cried, "There is still hope!" He picked up the ring, the jug, and the sack, and set off at once to find the golden castle.

He wandered about the dark wood until he could no longer find his way. When he grew tired, he lay down beneath the bushes and went to sleep. The next morning, he continued his wanderings. Day after day, he stumbled through the thick forest, and night after night, he slept beneath the bushes.

Then one night, he saw a light that seemed to be coming from the deepest part of the wood. He followed the light, and came to a house in which two giants lived. Boldly, he walked inside.

One of the giants seized him and roared, "My stomach is empty, but I will make a good supper of you!"

"That may be," said the young man. "But in my sack is something that would taste much better." Then he took out the jug and opened his sack. The giant sat down next to him, and they ate until they could eat no more.

When they were finished, the young man turned to the giant and said, "I am on my way to the golden castle. Can you tell me where it is?"

"I cannot say," replied the giant, "but my brother is sure to know."

At that very moment, the house began to rumble and shake, and the giant's brother came into the room. The young man offered him food and drink, and then asked him about the golden castle.

The second giant thundered, "I must look at my charts!" And he took out some huge maps. After studying them for some time, he said, "The golden castle is in a faraway land, but I will take you part of the way." Then he lifted the young man to his shoulders and strode out the door and through the dark wood.

When he finally stopped, the giant lowered the young man to the ground, saying, "I have done all I can. Now you must finish your journey alone."

So the young man continued on, traveling both day and night, until he finally came to the golden castle. It stood on top of a glass mountain that was so slippery no one could climb it. Each time the young man tried to reach the top, he slid back down to the bottom. So he built a small hut at the foot of the mountain, and vowed to wait there until the raven came down to him.

One morning the young man awoke to hear three robbers arguing outside his hut. "Have mercy!" he cried, and the arguing stopped for a moment. When it began again, he called out, "Have mercy!" and the arguing stopped again. But soon the robbers were fighting still louder than before.

It seems that the first robber had a stick that could open any door simply by tapping on it. The second had a cloak that could make anyone who wore it invisible. The third had a horse that could gallop over anything—even a glass mountain. But the robbers could not agree to keep these things for themselves, or share them with one another.

"Let me make a suggestion," offered the young man. "Each of you should have what he deserves, and I will gladly help you to decide. But first, I should try these things, to be sure they work as you say." So the robbers let him mount the horse, take the stick, and wear the cloak for a moment.

As soon as he had all three things, the young man began beating the robbers with the stick, saying, "There! Now each of you has got what he deserves!" Then he turned and rode the horse straight up the glass mountain to the golden castle. The gates were locked, but when he tapped them with the stick, they swung wide, and he passed through.

As soon as he entered the golden castle, the enchantment was broken, and the raven turned back into a Princess. She looked around to see who had broken the spell. But of course, she could not see the young man, whose cloak had made him invisible.

He took out the ring the raven had given him, and slipped it on the Princess' finger. At once she cried out, "Oh! If this is truly my golden ring, then I know who has broken the enchantment. But where is he? I do not see him."

Then she searched the golden castle, looking in every room and behind every door. But though she passed the young man many times, she never saw him. She was about to search the castle

again, when he suddenly threw off the cloak and became visible.

Tears of joy filled their eyes as they flew into each other's arms.

Of course, they were married the very next day. They moved into the golden castle, where they lived happily ever after.